CASTING
THE GODS
ADRIFT

CASTING
THE GODS
ADRIFT

GERALDINE
McCAUGHREAN

BLOOMSBURY EDUCATION

LONDON   OXFORD   NEW YORK   NEW DELHI   SYDNEY

For Rebecca van der Vliet

BLOOMSBURY EDUCATION
Bloomsbury Publishing Plc
50 Bedford Square, London, WC1B 3DP, UK
29 Earlsfort Terrace, Dublin 2, Ireland

BLOOMSBURY, BLOOMSBURY EDUCATION and the Diana logo are
trademarks of Bloomsbury Publishing Plc

First published in Great Britain 1998 by A & C Black,
an imprint of Bloomsbury Publishing Plc

This edition published in Great Britain 2005 by Bloomsbury Publishing Plc

A catalogue record for this book is available from the British Library

ISBN: PB: 978-0-7136-7455-2; ePDF: 978-1-4081-8039-6; ePub: 978-1-4081-5278-2

10

Printed and bound in Great Britain by CPI Group (UK) Ltd, Croydon CRO 4YY

To find out more about our authors and books visit
www.bloomsbury.com and sign up for our newsletters

Contents

Contents

1

A Boatful of Monkeys

I know what made me careless. It was the thought of seeing a god – in person – breathing, speaking, eating, moving about. Priests had worshipped at his shrine every day for two years. Now *I* was going to see him in the flesh – the pharaoh. God on Earth. The thought filled my brain. How could I think about anything else? So you see, it was all my fault.

Our ship, when we set sail that day, was a wonder to see. Even I was amazed, and I was accustomed to my father's trade. My father, Harkhuf, dealer in rare beasts, was himself a rare, golden creature in my eyes. Mostly away in the south – beyond a dozen white-water cataracts of the Nile, beyond the southernmost districts of Egypt, beyond even Nubia – Father would reappear once or twice a year, his clothes threaded with strands of the fur of leopard, cheetah and lion. He took wild animals and tamed them into purring house pets for mayors and noblemen and, of course, for the pharaoh.

'Pharaoh Amenhotep, may his names be spoken for ever, relied upon me completely for baboons,' he used to say, cocking his nose in the air and sniffing.

Baboons were always Father's favourite. Well, he was born in Hermopolis, and the people down there worship Thoth the baboon-god above all the rest. Pharaoh Amenhotep loved the beasts, too. So our home was always leaping with baboons, caged or tame, and little bronze figurines of baboons crouched in the living room. All the time I was growing up, they grinned at me, or bared their teeth – I never quite knew which.

Now the new pharaoh, son of Amenhotep III, had commanded my father to bring him animals; lots of animals, he said, for his new capital city. When word reached Father, he was breathless with delight. Despite my aunt's objections – 'Tutmose has his studies,' and 'Oh, surely you won't take Ibrim on the river!' – he invited my brother and me to go with him on the journey down the Nile to deliver the animals. 'The trip of a lifetime,' he said.

A lifetime, yes.

So, we set sail from Nehkeb in the *Palm of Thoth*, its decks laden with cages containing baboons, some smaller monkeys, a few serval cats and three dozen scarlet ibises. There were six baby crocodiles in a wooden trough, and two hunting falcons tethered to their perches with lengths of leather. The noise was cacophonous.

Father posted me in the prow to keep watch for sandbars. The river currents shift so much sand and mud about that the navigation channels are constantly changing. The hippopotami can wreck a boat, too. The holy Nile is a treacherous river, and boats have to be so shallow to sail it that they are quite frail.

My brother Ibrim sat up on the deckhouse roof, chanting the spell against crocodiles –

we never cross water without saying it – and playing his harp. Ibrim was losing his sight, you see. He had river blindness. Not unusual. Terrible, but not unusual.

My father would keep saying, 'You'll get better, son. Your eyes are improving every day.' But even then, young as we were, Ibrim and I knew it wasn't true. Father just wasn't very good at coping with bad news. He made sacrifices to the goddess Ishtar. He went on pilgrimages. He hung a gold case around Ibrim's neck. Inside it was a little rolled-up note from the great baboon-god Thoth, promising to protect him. Even so, I had to keep look-out on my own for sandbars, while Ibrim sat on the cabin roof. He had a sweet voice; I loved to hear him sing. But that day, all I could hear was the rush of water under the prow, and the baboons jabbering. All I could think about was seeing a god.

The broad sail was furled; we were travelling with the current. Even so, the northerly wind was blowing so strongly that we made slow headway. The rowers had to pull without rest on their oars. It occurred to me that, with our cargo of livestock, we must look like the Ship of a Million Days that sails the skies crowded with its animal-headed gods. I had seen pictures; their boat had the same upward curve at prow and stern, like the curve of a hammock; it had the same two great steering boards at the back, the same oars moving with perfect symmetry. I remember wondering if the gods were looking down just then, over the side of their ship, watching us sail the holy Nile, sail down the length of the Black Land, between banks bright with flax and wheat, gardens, orchards and vineyards, square white houses and little moored reed-boats.

'Is the Ship of Heaven made of reed, like this one, Father?' I asked.

'No. Cedarwood. Like the pharaoh's barge,' he answered at once.

In those days, I thought he knew everything about the gods.

As we sailed past Iunet, he pointed out the Temple of Hathor, goddess of birth and far-off lands, of gold and silver and music.

'She's protected me on all my travels,' said

Father proudly. 'On the way back we shall visit the temple and ask the priests to perform a ritual for Ibrim and bathe his eyes in the sacred water; let him sleep nearby and dream a cure for himself. I promise! On the way home.'

'She gave me my gift of music,' Ibrim said softly, from his perch on the roof. 'Perhaps I shouldn't ask for more.'

But Father chose not to hear.

We sailed only when there was daylight. The river, with its shifting mudbanks and shoals of sand, was too dangerous in the dark. As we sailed past Thebes, Father described the wonders of the Temple of Karnak there – nearly eight hundred lionesses carved in black granite, and the avenue of sphinxes, a sacred lake, gateways taller than twenty men. 'A hundred thousand people work here, Tutmose,' he said. 'Many of my animals live here.'

I thought he had been everywhere, seen everything, my wonderful father.

But, he had not sailed downstream beyond Thebes – not for twenty years. Pharaoh Amenhotep III had kept court at Thebes.

The new pharaoh had shifted ground. So on we sailed, past Thebes and Luxor. The further we sailed, the quieter Father became, lost in thought, contemplating his first meeting with Amenhotep's son. The new king. The new god on earth, ruler over all Egypt. There were strange rumours spreading up and down the Nile. The new pharaoh had changed more than his capital city; he had also changed his name – to Akhenaten (Spirit of Aten).

I, too, was lost in thought. What did a god look like? Would he speak to me? What should I say if he did? The sun was harsh on the moving water, hot on my shaven head, my naked body. I screwed my eyes shut against the brightness. I closed them, but my lids still glowed red. I covered my aching eyes with my hands.

And that was when we struck the sandbar.

2

Ship of Heaven

The rowers fell on their backs, cursing and struggling to keep their oars from slipping away into the river. I was thrown flat along the prow. The reeds scratched my face. From stem to stern, cages fell over and lay at crazy angles in the bottom of the boat, the animals inside shrieking and screaming. Ibrim slid, yelling, off the deckhouse roof and landed on the rush baskets full of bird seed. The small monkeys clung to one another, round-eyed, baring their sharp little teeth. The falcons' perches snapped and hung over the side like broken branches. The reed bundles which made up the *Palm of Thoth* crackled and crumpled upwards as she settled harder and harder aground.

On the distant riverbank, a single mould-green crocodile raised its grisly head and stared. Its angular legs took a few sidling steps and it sank from sight under water until only its upper jaw showed. *Splash*. *Splash*. There were others coming.

My father stumbled along the boat, stepping over the fallen rowers. I was expecting him to shout and rage at me, but he was too busy soothing and shushing the animals. The rowers were glaring at me, shouting prayers and reciting the crocodile spell. But father went on righting cages, apologising to the animals, hardly noticing as they bit the fingers gripping their cages. The cheetah was a ball of golden muscle and fur, clawing at her cage, chewing at the slats, spitting and arching her back into a shape as unnatural as the broken boat's. The ibises, in a cage by my feet, were beating themselves ragged against their bars, against each other, handfuls of slender feathers bursting out around my ankles.

'Let them go, fool! Let them go!'

I realised Father was speaking to me, telling me to unlatch the cage and loose the beautiful birds he had so painstakingly trapped, before they broke all their wings or drowned along with the boat. I did it.

The ibises burst out around me, battering my face with their scarlet wings, so that my world turned red. They fountained into the sky, piping shrilly. But the tethered falcons were past help. They were being pulled under the water as the boat settled lower. Their struggles brought the crocodiles in, slowly, glidingly. They were in no hurry. Their feast would not escape them; this basket of assorted meats that was gradually breaking up in front of their noses.

Father opened cages with trembling, hasty hands. 'Hold on, Ibrim!' he told my brother. 'Get up higher, boy! Good boy!' But he went to help the animals first. The reeds that made up the deepest part of the boat were sodden now, awash with river water. One by one, he opened the cages. His baboons lumbered out to sit on the sides of the boat, feet tucked up, backs hunched, long arms dangling, like miserable old men.

The crew would not let father loose the cheetah. They threatened to knock him overboard if he so much as went near the frenzied beast. Bad enough to drown, without being savaged, mid-river, by a wild cat. The boat shivered and hissed, and began to break apart.

Suddenly, a shadow flowed over us all like spilt ink, and a ship twice our size glided alongside. Had the Ship of Heaven indeed been watching us from the sky and swooped down to help us? I truly thought it had.

The baboons leaped in huge elegant bounds over our heads and into the rescue ship. The crew scrambled clumsily to safety over its smooth, painted sides. I edged my way round to where Ibrim was clinging to the steering paddle, and with my arm around his shoulders waited for help. 'Don't cry,' I said. 'Don't cry.' Only afterwards did I realise it was I, not he, who was crying.

Two oars, painted blue with pure white blades, reached out to us from the other vessel. I wrapped Ibrim's arms tight around one and, hugging the other myself, was lifted out of the *Palm of Thoth* by a huge, black-skinned, Nubian steersman. As I crossed the yawning gap, I looked down and saw a crocodile open the yellow shutter of an eye, startled to be robbed of his meal.

My father, too, was offered an oar's end to lift him clear. But he refused to be rescued until he had opened every cage, loosed every animal. At last, with his feet splashing through black, silty water, sinking deep into the fabric of the boat, he struggled aft towards the cheetah. But in her panic and fury, she hurled herself at him, overturning the cage which rolled through a gaping split in the boat and sank out of sight into the river. Crocodiles moved in under the hulk. Only then did my father allow himself to be lifted to safety with the blue-and-white oars.

The top-spar of the beautiful rescue ship was now alive with baboons swinging by their hands and feet, grimacing at the people below. I saw several little girls huddled together in the prow, pointing up at them and laughing uncertainly. The ship's rowers were now easing the barge upstream, away from the sandbar, leaving the *Palm of Thoth* foundering in midstream like a bale of straw pulled apart by rats.

Rather than watch ours sink, I looked

around at the boat that had come to our rescue. The deckhouse was more sublime than most houses I had ever seen on shore, with blue-and-white chequered walls and a gold-leaf balustrade. At the door stood a man and woman, hand in hand. They could have been westerners – spirits from the Land of the West where the fortunate go when they die. Their clothes were of gauzy white linen, and they wore jet-back wigs and amulets of gold and silver.

But they were not spirits, of course. They were gods. For we were aboard *The Splendour of Aten*. We had been redeemed from drowning by its captain, the god-king himself. 'Lie down on your face and pray,' I whispered to Ibrim. 'We are in the presence of the pharaoh!'

3

The Great House

I think my father was more afraid now than with the crocodiles gaping after him. He was in the presence of the pharaoh, watching the pharaoh's shipment of animals disappear into the boiling brown turmoil of the sandbank. He fell down along the deck, his face pressed against the boards, his breath breaking from him in little sobs of abject terror.

But, to his astonishment, the pharaoh bent down and raised him to his feet. 'Never fear, man, never fear! Give thanks to almighty Aten that he preserved you from the crocodiles!'

'But your animals—' blurted Father.

I could see the imprint of the cedarwood

deck on his cheek.

'There are always more animals. Calm yourself. Your children are safe. Is that not more reason to celebrate than to grieve? They are your sons, I take it?' He laid his hand on my shaven head – a god's hand on my head! – and ordered the rowers to pull away into the wider river, away from the sights and sounds of the sandbank.

We sailed on downstream, towards the distant white cubes of el-Amarna.

'Ah yes! Harkhuf! Your name is known to me!' said the pharaoh genially. 'You did great service to my father.'

'May his name live forever,' said Father.

'I hope you will fetch *me* many animals too. The queen and I are very fond of animals, and so are my daughters. Monkeys and cats, for preference. My daughters are particularly fond of cats.'

I snatched a glance at the little girls who had come to the doorway of the stateroom, dressed in linen so gauzy thin that they seemed to be wearing clouds. I gasped at the sheer beauty of them. Their pleated skirts were clasped at the hip with gold, and each

21

girl wore a collar of lapis lazuli.

'And birds for my aviary, yes!' the pharaoh was saying. 'I love their colours and their song... That reminds me. Did I hear singing from your boat, before she struck the sandbar? Was it you, boy?'

He turned to me a face more like a woman's than a man's, a wig of extraordinary curly hair bunching out from under his plumed headdress.

The smile was so encouraging, I stopped trembling in the instant. 'That was my brother, Ibrim! I can't sing a note!'

'Tutmose is a worthless boy,' agreed my father.

'Ah, but you are surely good at something?'

Now the *queen* was speaking to me. Day of days! A god and a goddess speaking to me! I was so overwhelmed that Ibrim had to answer for me.

'Tutmose is a great maker of things. He is clever with his hands! Clay models. Wood carvings. Just wonderful! Last year he made me a little elephant... I don't see very well, but even by touch I can tell—'

'Ibrim, be silent!' hissed my father, horrified by our temerity.

'Then there is a place for you all, at el-Amarna, it seems,' said the pharaoh. 'Wash off that Nile mud, good Harkhuf. We shall soon be reaching the quay.'

Nubian slaves brought bowls of clean water, and we washed. I bent my face over a washing bowl, and when I looked up again, I saw el-Amarna slipping up to meet the boat. It looked just as if it had dropped from the sky an hour before – a city of pale clay buildings, all new, all clean, all perfect. Huge pylon gateways, palaces and silos of stored grain all soared towards the burning blue sky. Squatting around them were smaller, cube-shaped houses, and everywhere there was colour and noise and movement and smells enough to make my head spin.

In a bakery, a man was taking honey cakes out of a clay oven. A dwarf was walking a pair of pet dogs along the shore. A row of bronze axe heads caught the sun – for sale outside a metalworker's shop. In every house yard, incense trees cast little pools of shade where cats slept, old men snoozed, or women sat washing lentils or chopping leeks. Naked children ran about playing leapfrog or football, or towing little toys about on string. The smoke from the cooking fires rose up to mingle with steam from freshly washed clothes. Men with brick-red skin were building yet more soaring walls of brick, while in the dark houses pale-skinned women stayed hidden from the sun's ferocious heat.

We seemed to be expected to follow the royal family, so we did – up one of the vast smooth ramps which led to doors high in the palace walls. Through countless anterooms, the pharaoh led us through his pharaoh – his 'great house'. I remember thinking how strange it was to call a king a 'great house'; but then I suppose a pharaoh does afford his people shelter and safety, so in that way he is like a house. We passed through a hall with, oh, fifty pillars holding up a painted ceiling. Then we were on the King's Bridge, on top of the city's gateway, in a covered walkway with a view right over el-Amarna. The pharaoh stopped and so did we.

'Welcome, my friends,' he said. 'Welcome to the city of Aten, the *only* god.' He turned to one of the courtiers who bobbed along in his wake like seagulls behind a plough. 'Take my animal collector to a temple where he can ask the priests to give thanks to Aten. Then find him somewhere to live. Tutmose here is to study handcrafts; the blind one is to study music under the royal musicians.'

'Oh, but my son isn't—' Father wanted to explain how Ibrim was not blind – far from it! He wanted to say how his eyes were getting better every day. But he dared not contradict the king.

'We greatly prize music here,' said Queen Nefertiti, resting the tips of her fingers on Ibrim's shoulder. 'You must not fear the dark, Ibrim. Aten shines into every life, in some way.'

Then the king's courtier led Father, Ibrim and me over the King's Bridge and directly to the Temple of Aten the sun. The courtier told us it was not like any other temple. It was not some gloomy secretive cave of a building, with looming statues and inner rooms where the priests communed mysteriously with images of the gods. This temple was open to the sun. 'There are no roofs to the temples of Aten. They are open to the rays of Aten, as every heart is open to His eyes,' said our guide in a bored, slightly routine way, as if he had said it many times before. He told us that the altars – there were many of them, either to Aten or to the divine pharaoh himself – were piled with fruit and flowers, and the walls were painted with the rays of the sun, each ray ending in a hand. I could feel the sun shining on the top of my head. I could feel the painted hands emptying blessings on my head. I was going to be a craftsman – a sculptor! – a maker of beautiful things for the beautiful daughters of Akhenaten! I was the happiest boy alive.

'But where are the other temples?' said Father, and there was a strange, strained quality to his voice. 'My boys must ask the priests to perform a thanks-offering ritual to the great baboon-god Thoth. Their life is preserved by the goodness of Thoth.'

'There is no god but Aten the sun,' said our escort, haughty as an ostrich. 'There are no other temples in el-Amarna. Aten the sun and our own god-king Akhenaten rule here. Is the news so slow to travel throughout their kingdom?'

'I had heard something of the kind,' said my father guardedly.

'So it shall be, as it is here, from end to end of the Nile. One god, just as there is one sun.'

Ibrim took hold of my hand. The floor was patterned, and he did not feel safe walking across it, for fear there were steps he could not see. 'I want to ask a priest to put an offering on his altar. On Akhenaten's altar,' he whispered to me. I could see from his face that he was as happy as I at the way things were turning out. 'But I only have the elephant you gave me. Everything else was lost with the boat.'

'Give it,' I said, brimming over with joy. 'I can make you something else. Soon I'll be able to make you *anything*! I'll be the best craftsman in all Egypt!' I led him over to a priest, and Ibrim took the elephant out of a little shoulder bag which hung, still river-sodden, against his dry clothes. We asked if it could be laid, with two figs, on an altar to Akhenaten.

On the wall beside us, a huge depiction of the pharaoh looked benignly down upon us. He was wearing the full panoply of kingship; the blue cobra crown, the crook and flail of kingly power crossed on his chest. The face looked pleased, gratified.

The heat bounded off the high, bright walls, redoubling like an echo. We sweated joy, my brother and I.

No more than a few steps from the temple, the courtier jerked his head abruptly at a house. 'You may stay here, since it is the pharaoh's wish,' he said grudgingly and, duty done, he scurried back to the palace.

'Isn't it wonderful, Father?' I burst out, dancing around, shaking my hands in the air. 'Music for Ibrim, and I shall be a sculptor! In the pharaoh's own workshops!' But even as I said it, I knew that somehow I was throwing straws on a fire, fuelling my father's rage, making his eyes bulge with pent-up fury.

Father was not overjoyed. He was on the verge of cursing or bursting into tears.

4

Man of Gold

'What? Am I to collect animals to decorate a room? To entertain babies? For slaves to walk them on a lead?'

Ibrim pressed himself against me. I put an arm around his shoulders, but we were reeds in front of a howling wind. I had never seen my father so angry.

'Are there to be no temples for my crocodiles? Are my baboons to be given no sacred burial?'

Ibrim began to whimper. Foolishly, I said, 'I don't know, Father.'

He bent down to yell into my face, 'My animals are the embodiment of the gods! Does this serpent-demon think he can overturn the Ship of a Million Days? Does he think to cast the gods adrift – to spill them back into the ocean of nothingness and drown them? His father, Amenhotep, may his name live for ever, was chosen by the gods to be pharaoh over Egypt! And does his son deny that the gods exist?' His hand reached out and snatched hold of the gold case strung around Ibrim's neck. 'If there is no Thoth, what good is this promise, eh? Who is protecting your brother's life? Eh? Eh?' And he let go so violently that the talisman flew up and hit Ibrim on the forehead.

I barely understood what he was talking about – only that this same Akhenaten who, with a word, had made my dreams come true, loosed some terrible nightmare on my father. The god-king so eager to employ him was a traitor to his own kind. Father had no choice but to serve the new pharaoh. He was a god, after all. But as a believer in the many other gods – Hathor, Khon, Thoth, Anubis, Osiris, Amun-Ra – he was bound by religious duty to hate Pharaoh Akhenaten with all his might.

'That's no reason to be angry with us,'

I snivelled, after he had stalked away into the house and we could hear him kicking the furniture.

'He's not angry,' said Ibrim, one hand closed round the golden talisman, the other against his forehead. 'He's scared.'

Of course I told him he was a fool and said what did he know, and that he was too young to understand. But I knew he was probably right. Ibrim always is about things like that.

Things soon righted themselves, for Father did not have to stay. We never had to suffer his terrible moods for long. He was always so soon gone again, south, upriver into Nubia and beyond, collecting more rare animals, trapping gorgeous birds. We stayed behind in el-Amarna this time, instead of going back to our old house. We did not miss our nagging, crabbed aunts. And we were happy.

Do you think that's strange? Do you think we should have been wondering and fretting about the number of gods in Heaven? Are you mad? We were boys. Little boys.

Ibrim learned the seven-stringed harp and the hand lyre, and then he discovered the Syrian lyre. It was taller than he was, and had *eight* strings. But he took mastery of it like a man taking mastery of a syrup tree, and soon he could fetch music out of it sweeter than syrup.

Me, I studied in the royal workshops. I was quick to learn – hungry to learn. Around me, everything was being made – the city sprawling outwards from the five palaces, the temples of Aten, the statues, the vases, the paintings were all new. There was a continuous noise of building, and the air was full of stonedust. A feeling of new opportunities existed here. Not like the feeling you get at Memphis, where the greatest achievements – the pyramids, the sphinxes, the colossal statues – were all made hundreds of years ago by people long dead; or at the Great Temple of Amun in Karnak.

Perhaps because of the dramatic way we had met the pharaoh, he seemed to take a particular interest in Ibrim and me. We were allowed to play inside the palaces, so long as we did not enter the women's quarters, and he even let us see the green room, where all the walls are painted to resemble the reed marshes, with birds flying upwards, and a pool painted on the floor. It was breathtaking.

The third oldest of the princesses, Ankhesenpa-aten, was an artist, too, and she would sometimes come to the workshop to see things being made. I was the youngest person there, so I suppose she found it easiest to talk to me.

'I like to paint,' she told me, looking at me with her almond-shaped eyes, lids painted the same colour as the green room. 'Mix me some paints, won't you?' And she set the ivory palette down in front of me. She could have asked me to cut out my heart and lay it on the palette. I would have done it without a murmur. She was the most beautiful creature I ever saw (apart from Queen Nefertiti herself).

But I was better at painting than Ankhesenpa-aten. That was where our friendship began – with me teaching her how to use the little palm-fibre brush. We used to sit together on one of the cushioned window seats of the palace and talk about pigments and kohl, and which animal's hair could be used for brushes, and whether there were any paintings in the West Country, the country on the other side of Death.

Consequently, I saw everything in their palace – the golden beds, the sunken baths and lavatories, the alabaster vases, the banqueting tables. We gorged on sweet figs, dates and pomegranates, and I told Ankhesenpa-aten my secrets and she told me hers. I think I must have told her even more than I told Ibrim (though I never spoke of Father and his rages). She tended to help herself to the things I had made, but I was more pleased than annoyed; it was a kind of praise. I thought I would be happy for ever.

From time to time, Father arrived with a shipment of monkeys and cats and birds – and the whole royal family would gather to gaze out of the palace windows, the little princesses (there were six) pointing and squealing and the great queen laughing, and Father breaking off from checking his inventory to bow in their direction every now and then. I would see Pharaoh Akhenaten congratulate him, lay a hand on his shoulder and admire Father's genius in capturing such splendid specimens. Father's birds fluttered around the courtyard aviary of the Great Palace, and brought joy to the pharaoh every time he stopped to admire them.

No one had forced Father to abandon his gods. True, there were no temples to Thoth or the creator-god Amun-Ra in el-Amarna. But further along the river, all the old religious customs were still being carried out, all the temples and shrines and places of pilgrimage still existed. Most of Egypt was going on as it had always done, its priests worshipping the same gods as their forefathers. Akhenaten had not banned the worship of other gods. So I could see no reason for my father to fret. None in the world.

When I had mastered fine chisel work, I was put to work making cartouches – ovals with hieroglyphs inside them spelling out a particular royal name. I was entrusted with the carving of the queen's cartouche – that's how good I was. A hundred times and more I carved that lozenge: *Nefernefruaten-Nefertiti – Beautiful are the Beauties of Aten – A Beautiful Woman is Come.* And never once did I carve it without thinking of the queen's face, more beautiful than any words, or any carving of a word.

Even the memory of my own mother, who died when Ibrim was born, is not as beautiful to me as the thought of Queen Nefertiti. So tender, so serene, so marvellous in her tall blue crown snaked round with a golden cobra. The king adored her – carried her in his chariot when he rode out into the desert; took her in his papyrus skiff down to the reed marshes; shared his glory equally with her when he was carried shoulder-high through el-Amarna on a palanquin of dazzling electrum, fanned with ostrich-feather fans.

The whole world was in awe of the pharaoh and his great queen that year, and I more than anyone. Father brought home from Assyria a tamed lion, with fur of pale gold and a mane of black flecked with silvery gold. Electrum the Lion, we called it.

Pharaoh Akhenaten walked the beast on a red leather leash through the five palaces, beaming with satisfaction as he did so. Then he stroked my father on the back (as one might a lion) and told him, 'For this and for all your loyal efforts, I shall make you a Man of Gold!'

I thought nothing could ever cloud my happiness. What did it matter if there was one god or a whole shipful? My father was to be a Man of Gold, the highest honour conferred on an official of the pharaoh's court. Surely even father must be won round by such an honour?

On the day of the ceremony, the two oldest princesses stood by their father holding golden collars piled on a scarlet cushion. Ankhesenpa-aten held a golden tray, and stood on the other side of the throne. As each chosen Man of Gold approached the dais, a herald spoke aloud the great service they had done to the pharaoh and to Aten. The king presented the collars, and the queen took from the golden tray a pair of red leather gloves, and presented them as well.

I had to describe it all to Ibrim; his sight had left him altogether now and plunged him into a sunless dark full of music and incense and the noise of building. But despite his blindness, he was happy that day. Who would not be?

'What did he say to you, Father? What did the pharaoh say?'

The collar of gold strips hinged with leather seemed to weigh heavily on Father, hollowing his chest, rounding his shoulders. 'He offered me a boon. Any boon within his power to grant.'

'What did you ask for, Father?' said Ibrim, leaping up and down, hanging on to one scarlet-gloved hand.

'I asked to attend the Festival of Opet with my family.'

I knew it, of course I did. It was a big religious festival. But I felt a clammy hand grip my guts. It was not the most tactful thing my father could have asked for, after all – to attend a festival in honour of a god other than Aten. 'Oh, and did he grant it?' I asked.

'He says there will be no Festival of Opet

this year,' said Father, in a voice I did not recognise – choked, almost strangled to a whisper. 'Nor even the Festival of Osiris. He is closing down the temples of all the gods but Aten the sun.'

Even I was shocked. What would happen if Akhenaten succeeded in driving the gods out of Heaven? Wouldn't times of catastrophe and disaster begin? I automatically threw a nervous glance towards the river. I couldn't help it. That was where Set lived, the demon-hippopotamus bent on devouring Egypt. Without the god Horus to subdue him with magic harpoons, wouldn't Set surface and begin to devour my world? Would Osiris, unworshipped, withdraw his gift of life-after-death and refuse to receive the souls of those who died? Would the great snake Apep beneath the earth rear up its head one day soon, to see the Ship of a Million Days floating by empty, adrift, no one aboard. For the first time, I tasted some of the fear that had been tormenting my father.

'All Egypt is to worship Aten as the only

god,' Father was saying, his voice shrill with sarcasm. 'It is the will of Aten. That is what he said to me.' He was a man bereft. His gods had been turned out-of-doors, exiled, cast adrift in their open boat to die. I saw there were tears in his eyes. I saw how he raised a hand to brush them away, and was met by the sight of a red glove.

If he had found a scorpion there, a finger's breadth from his face, I don't believe he would have reacted any differently. He flung his hand away from him so sharply that the glove flew through the air to land on a stack of drying bricks. I ran to fetch it and hugged it to me – a gift from a god to a mortal man. How many boys ever held such a thing? But when I went back to father and Ibrim, I held it out of sight, behind my back, so that Father should not have to take it back.

I had bad dreams that night. I had bad dreams many nights after that. I dreamed that I was in a reed boat, and a hippopotamus erupted out of the river ahead of me, gaping its mouth so wide I could see right down its gullet to the fires burning inside. I threw a harpoon, but it just glanced off the wet, black, rubbery hide, and the beast still came on, chewing up the prow with those blunt, stubby teeth, rending the boat into shreds to get at me, to devour me—

I woke up screaming, and my father came to me, his eyes unnaturally bright in the darkness.

'What did you dream, boy? *What*?'

Something kept me from telling him. I claimed that my nightmare had gone, in waking; he could not know any different. But I did want him to sit down on the edge of the bed, to stay and chat about nothing very much, until the fright left me – to show me I was safe in el-Amarna, in the house of a Man of Gold. He did indeed sit down on my bed, and lean his face down close to mine.

Then he whispered, 'Do you know what becomes of the servants of the enemies of the gods, boy? Do you? They die a second death and are eaten, through all eternity, by monsters in the Underworld.'

'I serve all the gods, Father! All of them! Truly!'

'Ah, but we all belong to Akhenaten, don't we? All Egypt belongs to Akhenaten. Every soul in it. He will take us with him, boy, I see it. The king will take us all down to the Underworld, you see if he doesn't. Monsters, boy! Foul monsters!'

With that he left me, stumping back to bed, muttering, chanting, praying; I don't know which.

Yes, I had a good many nightmares after that.

5

The Red Country

Some of the things made in the royal workshops were for the palaces: a bath lined in smooth limestone, hassocks for the seats, carved beds with legs like lion paws and gilded with gold leaf.

But most of the things we made were for the afterlife. It is not so hard for us mortals. We have little to call our own in this life, so we don't have to take much with us – a pair of sandals, a loaf of bread, a few beads, perhaps. But a pharaoh! He needs everything, and everything he needs must be perfect, beautiful, worthy of a god. All life long, his craftsmen must make things for his tomb: cups, skiffs, make-up, games, clothes, pets, crowns, musical instruments – everything.

Having so much treasured up, he then has to keep his treasure safe from thieves, and his tomb, as well as being a point of departure for the heavens, has to be secure. Even the mighty pyramids had not proved impregnable. Better to carve a tomb out of solid rock somewhere secret, somewhere no one but the sun's rays will find it. Akhenaten decided to build his tomb out in the Red Country, the desert beyond the green of the Nile valley.

The Red Country is a really sinister, scary place, unblessed by the holy Nile. Nothing chooses to grow there, and the wind raises spectral shapes out of the dust, like running men. Strange place to build a tomb, where everything sweet in life springs from the watered places. But that is where Akhenaten decided to build his 'House of Eternity'; his starting point for the journey to the afterlife. And we went with him, Father and I, the day he decided to visit the site. That's how trusted we had become.

We rode out in chariots, but the charioteer would not let me hold the reins. Father was fretful and tetchy. He kept saying, 'Why has he asked us? Why is he showing us this tedious place?' I was just anxious to hold the reins.

The Red Country was not for us, not for our family. Father had purchased a grave site at Abydos. Though it had cost him his life savings, and had to be kept secret from the king, he felt much, much safer now, knowing that in death, he was better provided for than the king. Abydos, city of tombs, had grown up on the banks of the Nile on the very spot where the goddess Isis magically raised her husband Osiris from the dead and taught mortals the secrets of eternal life. Anyone buried in Abydos will be raised to life just like Osiris. Of course only the richest can afford to be buried there, but even quite poor people set up stelae, burial posts carved with their names, so that Osiris won't forget them. No, this red, dusty place was not for us. Not Harkhuf's family.

But one day the Princess Ankhesenpa-aten would lie here. She too would have her House of Eternity alongside her father's, crammed with gold, silver, gems and ushabti cats. She was really excited to visit the place that morning. I hated the thought of it. I hated the thought of Ankhesenpa-aten growing old, or sick, or dying – being buried in her father's misguided religion, in this awful, blood-red place. In fact, I did my best to get all such thoughts out of my head, and busied myself thinking about better things. About chariots, chiefly.

In particular, I thought about the pharaoh's chariot. How would it be to ride in that? There it stood, leather and wood armoured all over with gold, with two black horses plumed and stamping. How glorious to tear along, the reins lashed round my waist like a real charioteer, over the desert and through the tape of the horizon, winning every race!

The last little bit of the way, the pharaoh, his daughters and his men of gold went on foot, not even shielded from the sun's heat by fan-bearers. The exact location of the tombs must remain a secret, for fear grave robbers might break in and steal the treasure which would one day be heaped around the king's sarcophagus. Not for me to know. Not for charioteers or fan bearers. I remained behind. I remember, Ankhesenpa-aten looked back over her shoulder and waggled her fingers at me as they walked away.

I wish I could buy you a grave at Abydos! I thought. Away from this ungodly place.

I looked at the king's chariot. His charioteer was busy talking to the other drivers. How could it hurt just to try?

Up I stepped, on to the running board. One of the horses turned his head and snorted. The charioteer looked round and brandished his whip at me.

The horses sprang straight from standing into a gallop. There was no time to jump off, no time to even think. The floor of the chariot seemed to be pounding my legs into my hips, jarring my kneecaps like hammer blows. I made a snatch at the reins, but they were tied to the chariot and not round my waist.

Foam from the horses' mouths came flying back and hit me in the face. Their black bodies creamed with instant sweat. I clung to the sides, but I was being pitched about like the clapper in a bell, and my legs were not long enough to brace against the leather panels.

Out over the red, cracked earth I hurtled, out over red earth crumbling away to sand and peppered with rocks. Past locust trees and thorn bushes and boulders shaped like skulls, away from the king's party, away from the river, straight into the Red Country where no Egyptian chooses to go.

My hold on the chariot could not last. When both wheels struck a rock, the front of the chariot reared up, and I went out of the back, heels-over-head, landing on my face. The horses galloped round in a wide arc and plunged back the way they had come. But they went without me.

I was left alone on the red earth, scalding hot against my palms and thighs. I dragged myself on to my hands and knees, got up and ran a few steps. But, suddenly, the whole blue dome of the sky was singing and mouldering over with patches of black. I put my hand up to flick an insect off my neck and found it was not an insect but a trickle of blood from inside my ear. I felt violently sick. The horizon sloped and doubled into two distinct lines. The ground lurched and I fell down again, not knowing how to get up.

Lying on my back, a prey to scorpions and snakes, I called open-mouthed for my father. But I could not hear my voice. So I called inside my head instead – called on every god whose name I could remember: on Thoth, on Isis, on Apis and Bast and Sobek.

But I knew, even as I called, that there were no gods in this place. It was empty, barren, scorched. As far as the eye could see, no living creature moved. There might be scorpions and snakes in the crevices of the cracked earth, but there was nowhere for a god to hide. Here was Death's country, and I was alone in it. Only one thing ruled here, and that was the sun. The pharaoh was right. Out here, on the edge of the universe, there was only Aten. Of course he was right. Was he not a god himself? And gods must know these things. I could feel his beams scorching my face. I could feel his magic boiling my blood. I could see his hands reaching down from the sky – flails of light, crooks of sunlight. Aten was the same here as over the town where I was born, or over el-Amarna, or over the cool reed marshes. He was everywhere; I could see that now. It was just that here he was plainer to see, closer to the earth.

I found myself praying aloud. 'O Aten, only ruler of Earth and Heaven; let me live, and I will worship you all the days of my life! O Aten, don't let me die – not here in the Red Country, all alone and unburied!'

The ground shook. A scorpion, walking slowly past my outstretched fingertips, paused, sting raised, at the vibration. I thought I was feeling the movements of the serpent Ipep under the earth, wrestling against the forces of light.

Then a shower of red dust blew over me, and a chariot thundered past, and the pharaoh's charioteer reined it in. The pharaoh himself came and leaned over me. I could not see his face with the midday sun blazing behind his head.

'There now, Tutmose. That will teach you not to overstep your mark.'

'There is only one god: Aten and Akhenaten his servant!' I said the words of

50

a prayer I had heard issue many times from the temples of Aten.

'That's right, little Tutmose. And you have put him to the trouble of saving your life twice over.' But his face looked only mildly amused, rather than angry.

His charioteer picked me up and carried me in his arms, bracing himself in the tail of the chariot while the pharaoh himself drove it back to the edge of the Red Country. The Nile valley glimmered greenly along the horizon, broken by the temples and pylon-gateways of el-Amarna.

Father looked pale to the point of sickness. I was touched by his concern for my safety, sorry he had been put to such long, courteous apologies. 'My son is a blight on my life ... a curse on my family name ... his mother's shame. I shall beat him soundly for being such a grain of sand in the pharaoh's eye...' On and on he went.

But I soon found out that it was not I who had offended my father, not I who had died out there in the desert. At the secret site of the royal tombs, among the grim red cliffs and the wastes of scree, Akhenaten had accorded his men of gold the ultimate honour. They, like the princesses, were to have tombs alongside his House of Eternity. Like it or not, Harkhuf was to sleep forever in the Red Country, under the eye of Aten the sun.

6

A Dream of Wickedness

I did not tell him. I did not even try. There was no point. A father can tell his son what to believe – for a while, at least – but a boy can't tell his father. I must have told Ibrim fifty times over when we got back and we were alone together, 'It's true! Everything the pharaoh tells us is true! There *is* only one Aten. I felt it. I felt Him! Out there in the Red Country!' And Ibrim nodded and pictured it in his head, and believed me, because I was his older brother and I had never deliberately told him an untrue thing.

But Father was a different matter. He left on a trip to Nubia the day after my adventure with the chariot. I was still confined to bed, with double vision and a

53

terrible headache. Not until my head cleared did the solution come to me. I knew how to bring back my father from the brink of despair. The means of doing it was in my own hands! *what he want to give his dad*

I would carve him a stela – a name post to set up at Abydos. So that wherever his mortal remains were laid to rest, Osiris, god of the West Country would know Harkhuf was a true believer and would raise him to everlasting life! It would be the most beautiful stela Abydos had ever seen. I had the skill in my hands to make it. And I owed it to my father. I loved him, and I wanted to give him something which would prove that – both to him and to me.

In every spare moment I worked on the carving, wrapping it in cloths between times, and hiding it away from prying eyes. I must not on any account betray my father as an unbeliever in Aten; that would have meant his ruin. I think it was the finest piece of work I ever did. When I needed encouragement I would let Ibrim run his sensitive fingers over it and he would say, 'Such detail! Such delicate work! It must be the finest piece of work you've ever done, Tutmose!' I could not wait for Father to come home so that I could give him my wonderful present.

I knew, of course, that the magic of Abydos was imagined. I knew that Aten was the only god over Egypt. But Harkhuf would be buried with the divine Akhenaten. So that was all right, wasn't it? That would keep him safe and grant him a happy afterlife. Time enough for him to find out his mistake, then, in the Country of the Westerners.

I treasured up my news, like Akhenaten amassing his treasure ready for the red tombs. The wait was long.

One day, a neighbour suddenly came running to tell me that my father's boat was docking at the quayside, with ostriches and a baby elephant, jackals and a dead zebra. I ran to greet my father. Of course I could not blurt out my surprise in a public place, but as soon as we were alone...

I expected to see Harkhuf as he had looked when he left – bent and broken and grey with misery. But he was transformed.

He was thinner, his movements were quick and sharp, his eyes bright as sparks from an axe, and his jaw muscles rigid. He seized me by the elbow and pulled me close to him – not in an embrace, but to whisper in my ear. 'I have news for you! Later. At the house.'

'So do I,' I said, grinning at the knowledge of my marvellous secret.

I never got the chance that day to mention the stela. At home, my father sent Ibrim to practice, and sat down, hard up against me on the couch, his eyes darting wildly right and left. He jumped up to check for eavesdroppers at the door, at the window, then returned to the couch.

'On my way home I stopped at Edfu, at the Temple of Hathor the Protector. I bathed in the holy springs.'

'Why? Are you ill?' My heart sank inside me. I knew he was still thinking of a cure for Ibrim, still hoping for Ibrim to recover his sight.

'For the sake of your brother, stupid! And that night I had a dream! I did! The plainest dream I ever dreamed in my life. The gods revealed themselves to me, Tutmose!'

A flicker of wonder and dread crept through me, for all my conversion to Aten. 'Was I in the dream?'

He could not hear me. 'One day, Tutmose, you must paint my dream on the wall of my tomb: Ibrim, his eyes big as cymbals, and the Criminal, and a great cobra—'

'A cobra?'

'I dreamed, Tutmose, that Ibrim was cured – was perfectly whole again. I dreamed of Akhenaten sitting on his throne. And rearing up over him was a hooded cobra in the very act of striking!'

I was almost disappointed. 'That's his crown, Father. The triple crown with the cobra coiled around, rearing up to strike. And Ibrim *is* made whole. He's happy. Didn't you hear him tell you down at the quay? He plays now for Queen Nefertiti herself; in the royal orchestra! He's very happy.' I might as well have been talking underwater.

'Don't you see what it means, Tutmose?' said my father, grasping my shoulders, almost breathless with delight. 'The gods are calling for vengeance on their detractor!

They want Akhenaten destroyed! And we
must do it for them!'

7

The Nile-blue Cat

Out of a soft reed pannier Harkhuf pulled a wooden box, and set it down on the bench where we ate our daily food. Then he pulled on the scarlet gloves – those detested gloves that the pharaoh had presented to him, and lifted off the box lid.

I thought they were eels at first, wriggling around, knotting and unknotting. Then I realised. They were snakes – deadly poisonous Nile asps.

'No, Father. You can't,' I breathed. 'How can you kill a god?'

'Isis did.' He had his answers well rehearsed; he had been over and over them so often in his overheated brain. 'The goddess Isis made a snake to poison Amun-

Ra himself, ha ha! Poisoned the father of all the gods! That was how she won herself a place on the Ship of a Million Days!'

I wanted to say, 'There is no god but Aten. There never was an Isis or a magic snake. It's a story, a myth.' But I did not. I said, 'But Isis cured Amun-Ra afterwards. How will you cure the pharaoh?'

The light of madness was in his eyes.

'I shan't! No one shall! Monsters will tear at him in the Underworld, from everlasting to everlasting. But *you*, Tutmose, *you*!'

'*Me?*'

How was I to be involved in this insane scheme? Was I to be a part of it, this blasphemy, this plot to kill a god?

'What are you making at the moment? For the Great Criminal Akhenaten. At the workshop.'

I shrugged. 'A cat. A cat in blue faience.'

'Bast. The cat goddess. Very good.'

'No, no,' I insisted. 'Just a blue cat. For Pharaoh Akhenaten's tomb. He likes cats.' But Father was deaf to everything he did not want to hear.

'Excellent. Bast shall do it! It is fitting.'

He thrust his arm under mine and towed me, half-running, out of the house and towards the royal workshops, the box of asps tucked under his other arm. Outside the workshop door he said, 'Fetch it. Fetch the cat ... and clay to seal it.'

Such was my fear of those protruding eyes, those big blood vessels pulsing in his forehead, that crushing grip on my arm, that I did as I was told. 'It's not finished!' I protested. 'The eyes—'

'It's perfect.' He set down the box of asps and snatched the cat out of one of my hands and the ball of wet clay out of the other. In the shadow of a wall, wearing those blood-coloured gloves, he managed to tip a squirming knot of asps into the hollow figurine and stop up the base with a disc of unfired clay.

Then he spat in the dirt and made mud plugs to seal up the empty eye-sockets. Never once did he comment on the workmanship, on the luminescent blue glaze, on the expression of the cat that had cost me hours of patient effort. That was all I could think of at the time. My work of art was just a container to him, a vessel in which to package his venomous hatred. The gloves were ruined, too, caked brown and crisp with dirt.

'Now, all you have to do,' said Father, 'is to take it somewhere the Criminal will find it. Place it by his bed. The gods will help you.'

'*No!*' I could not help the word slipping out. It hung in the air between us, large as an apple. My mind was racing. If I refused to help, Father would make the attempt himself; he might even succeed. If I went along with the plan, I could at least make certain that it failed. Inside the cat, the asps were twisting themselves into infinite coils of wickedness. 'No, no. It's not perfect enough, Father! The base is just raw clay. It has to dry. Akhenaten would never believe a thing half-made like this was meant for him. Let me smooth it off and dip it in colour. Let me. Let me do the job properly. Let me, Father.'

We held the cat between us, me gently tugging, trying to ease it out of his grasp. 'It just needs a coat of paint. Let it dry and it's ready,' I said, wheedling. 'And the sun's going down. Soon the gods will be underground. Wait till morning when they're overhead – when they can see, and help and cheer.'

It was that picture of the gods hanging over the side of the Ship of a Million Days that won my father round. Like gamblers at a cockfight, he pictured them, cheering him on in his heroic murder. He let go of the blue-glazed cat, and I darted back into the workshop and set it down on my workbench.

I thought, if the kiln was hot, I would put it in there and kill the snakes. But the kiln was out, so I settled for standing the cat on my bench, under a sack. I would go back after dark when Father was asleep, and dispose of its lethal contents without him ever knowing. That way he might blame the gods, and not me, for letting him down.

The sun rested on the horizon, distorted to the shape of an ostrich egg. Aten-the-all-seeing was leaving the sky, leaving me alone with my father's wicked dream. This one night, I was terrified to see Him go. I would be without His help till morning.

Having kept his plan secret for weeks, my father now wanted to talk. He wanted to talk and talk and talk. Ibrim had gone to the palace to play at a banquet for a visiting Syrian diplomat; he would not be home till morning. Father felt free to talk to me, his fellow-conspirator. Though I doubt he had slept one night since his dream at Edfu, he showed no sign of weariness. A demonic energy kept him wide awake, whereas I could feel my eyelids drooping, my stomach aching for want of sleep. I never knew that *worry* could be so exhausting.

When I woke, the sun was well up. It took me a moment to remember that Father was home. Then I saw him, curled up like a baby on the couch, his face aged by years in the sun, the bones of his skull sharply white under the skin. Creeping on bare feet, so as not to wake him, I carried my clothes outside and dressed as I ran up to the workshop, through streets already crowded with people.

A half-dozen craftsmen, already seated at their benches, looked up as I opened the door of the workshop. At my own work

64

place, my tools lay ranged in an orderly row, like a surgeon's knives. Beside them lay a fold of sacking. Where the blue-glaze faience cat had stood there was a circle in the wood shavings, the spilled slip and scraps of clay. But the cat itself had gone.

Someone had taken it.

8

Song of the Reedbeds

'The cat! Where is the cat?' I blurted out at the man hammering gold leaf by the window.

'The princess took it,' he said with a wry smile, knowing how many times it had happened before.

'The princess? Are you sure? Did you see her?'

'Not a hundred breaths ago,' said the goldsmith, wincing at my loudness. He was understandably puzzled. I had never before objected to Ankhesenpa-aten helping herself. He cursed me as I threw open the door and made a draught that fluttered some of his golden flakes to the ground.

I ran after the princess, but did not catch

up before she reached the queen's palace, where I could not follow. I stopped in front of the guards, havering, uncertain what to do, picturing Ankhesenpa-aten, my exquisite 'Ankh', poking her little paintbrush into the caked eye holes, brushing them open. I thought of the asps glimpsing light and rearing up their little bulbous heads, licking the air, tasting the perfume of Ankh. Then I set off to run around the seemingly endless palace wall to where I knew Ankh's room looked out over an orchard of frankincense and moringa trees.

'Princess! Princess Ankhesenpa-aten!' I called in a whisper that quickly broke into a cry of desperation. 'Princess, *please*.'

At last, her sweet, oval face appeared, framed by the arch of the window. 'The cat, Princess! Did you take the cat?'

It was not seemly to suggest any such thing, I knew that. To suggest that a princess had filched something from a craftsman! By all the laws of courtesy, I should have pretended the cat never existed, or that I had given it to the princess myself, or that it was still in my workshop. The face at the window looked shocked.

'It was pretty.' She pursed her lips, preparing to be outraged if I dared to question her right to take it.

'It wasn't finished. It was only half made!' I protested. 'Let me have it back, and I'll make it perfect for you!'

'Was it not for me?'

'No. I mean, yes! Of course! Naturally! But you deserve only what is perfect! It has to be perfect for you... *Please*!'

'Well, it doesn't matter now. I have given it to my mother as a present.' And she pouted a little, for I had spoiled her presents as well as questioning her actions.

'Your *mother*! You gave it to the *great queen*?'

Ankhesenpa-aten turned away from the window. Her handmaid was waiting to make her ready for the public gaze. When I called again, she reappeared, impatient and angry with me, a cone of perfumed wax fastened to the crown of her glossy black wig.

'Princess, where is my brother? Have you seen him? I must find my brother!' I called up to her. Ibrim could find the cat, I told myself, and retrieve it since, as a musician, he was free to come and go within the palace.

'Your *brother*? How should I know?' She shrugged peevishly. 'On board the barge, I expect. We are going down to the reed marshes. The Syrian ambassador wishes to hunt. There will be musicians, I suppose. No *potters*, though.' She turned her back on me, haughty and serene in the face of my agitation.

I retraced my steps home, sunk in despair. I found Father singing as he washed, blithe and excitable as a child on the morning of a festival. I told him what had happened, and he was delighted. 'Aha! The queen bee carries the poison back to the hive and poisons all her drones! Excellent! Excellent!'

I crammed my anger away like a sail into a basket. Anger would not achieve anything. Instead, I took myself over to the Temple of Aten and asked the priests to perform a ritual prayer for me. '*O Aten, let her not die! Reach down your sunny hand and protect the divine family!*'

But I could not sit idly by and wait. If there was to be a boat trip to the reed marshes, the palace would be largely empty of people. I might just be able to get inside the royal quarters and find the cat. I went down to the quayside to watch the royal family embark – to make certain of them being out of the way.

The great cedarwood barge threw the shadow of its long, bowed shape across the waterfront, the river bubbling and hissing past the hull, the oarsmaster shouting orders to the crew. Under a canopy near the prow, I caught sight of Ibrim seated on a woollen cushion, with his hand lyre. I threw up my arms to catch his attention – forgetting his blindness. There was absolutely no chance of reaching him.

A crowd had gathered, as crowds always did, to see the king and queen. By the time I had pushed my way through to the front, Akhenaten, Nefertiti and the six princesses had come gliding down to the wharf and were climbing aboard, while the crowd called out blessings and praises, and bowed down reverentially.

I forgot to bow. My eyes were fixed on Queen Nefertiti, glorious in her blue crown banded with gold, her white linen wrapper, her golden sandals. In the crook of her arm, its eyes still plugged with clay, sat the little Nile-blue faience cat. She had brought her daughter's present with her from the palace!

Among the crowd, I saw my father's face, gloating, utterly delighted with himself. The royal barge pulled out from the quay, and around it a flotilla of little papyrus boats and coracles bobbed like lambs around a ewe. The faithful were always eager for a glimpse of the pharaoh, the living god.

An empty skiff bumped against the quayside at my feet. That was it! That was what I had to do – go after the royal barge! Father had to come, too.

Somehow, I plucked him out of the crowd and got him into the boat before he could refuse. He did not understand what he was doing there, and clung to the sides chanting the prayer against crocodiles and bleating dismally about my rowing.

Soon, most of the flotilla of little boats peeled off one by one, and turned back to el-Amarna, but I kept on plying the single oar at the stern, riding the current, riding the glossy wake which marked out the path taken by the royal barge.

Downstream, the reedbeds make a dark cage of stems against which everything is in silhouette, and colours merge into a single shadowy green haze. Widgeon and teal break cover and dart into the sky. There is a continuous singing throb of frogs, and the occasional bubbling up of gas from rotting vegetation below water. Bulrushes form, for mile upon mile, a guard of honour to the little boats which nose and butt among them. Mosquitoes drone, and fish nibbling at the reed stems set the brown velvet rush-tips swaying. There are water snakes, too.

Amidst this lovely turquoise world, Queen Nefertiti, the great queen, the beautiful one, cradled on her knees a faience cat that was aswarm inside with asps. A single bite from any one, and she would be dead within hours.

My papyrus skiff chafed and bumped against the moored barge. Some of the king's guests, mayors and Syrians, were disembarking into skiffs and starting to hunt for birds deep among the reedbeds. One man would stand in the prow with a handful of throwing sticks, knocking down birds scared out of hiding by slaves wading thigh-deep and slapping the water.

But the pharaoh did not disembark. The royal family did not hunt, never went hunting.

'What kind of man does not hunt?' sneered my father, and not for the first time. 'Look, son, can you see? He's half woman, that one, with his fat rump and his big—'

'*Be quiet, Father*!' I hissed. 'If he doesn't look like you and me, it's because he's half god.'

Harkhuf rose unwisely to his feet and came at me down the boat. I shouted for him to sit down. The skiff rocked wildly. He struck his head sharply against the beetling wooden hull of the royal barge, and sat down abruptly, stunned into silence. He looked up just as a handful of pomegranate seeds landed on his shoulder, apparently out of the sky.

The commotion had drawn attention to us. The pharaoh was leaning over the side, now, holding half a pomegranate; he hailed us genially. 'Harkhuf? Is it you? What brings you here?'

Father did not answer. Someone had to. Someone had to say something. I stood up. 'O King, we are ashamed to admit it!' I stammered. Father shot me a look of such hatred that I thought he might throw me to the crocodiles before the day was over. 'I told my father how Ibrim plays now for the great queen, the beautiful one. He wanted to hear for himself. Hear Ibrim playing in the pharaoh's presence, I mean. It was pride, O Lord King. Pride made us forget our manners and interrupt the peace of your afternoon!'

'Harkhuf, my old friend!' laughed the King. 'You had only to say! Come aboard, and we shall have music. Your son is indeed a credit to his father – both your sons!'

I thought my father might refuse, or blurt out something rash and insulting and fling himself into the river. I leaned forward, until my face was right in front of his. 'Get aboard, or I shall tell the pharaoh what you did last night.'

Bewildered and undermined, Harkhuf allowed himself to be helped aboard, once again over the bulwarks of the cedarwood barge. His eyes, blood-shot from the brightness of the journey downstream, flickered to and fro along the deck. He looked hunted, penned in, guilty, but the pharaoh mistook it for simple embarrassment.

At the sound of our voices, Ibrim sat bolt upright on the cushions in the prow of the boat, trying to make sense of what was happening, what we were doing there. Pharaoh Akhenaten sat down on his own silken cushion, put his arm around Nefernefruaten-Nefertiti. The six little princesses – among them my beautiful Ankh – sat behind, in descending order of size, the cones of perfumed wax melting into their hair and down their bare necks, shoulders, throats. That sweet scent mixed with my fear for their lives made my head spin. I spread my hands on the hot deck to steady myself as Akhenaten called for Ibrim to begin playing.

I don't know what he played – whether happy or sad, a love lament or a dance. My eyes and mind were on the Nile-blue pottery cat standing on the deck beside the queen's cushion. If I hurled myself towards it, I knew the bodyguard (although he stood at a discreet distance and looked half asleep) would snuff out my life as easily as snuffing out a candle.

The huntsmen had moved off deep into the rushes. The reedbeds were noisy again with their own droning music. But Ibrim's playing rose above it. He was happy. His music spoke happiness. And his happiness conveyed itself to the face of the great queen who, beautiful and serene as the Sphinx, watched him with cat-like concentration.

I looked sidelong at Father, and saw that he too had seen the faience cat. His eyes were fixed on it. His face was scarlet with the oppressive heat, and little beads of sweat were bursting through his wrinkled skin. Perhaps he was beginning to realise the enormity of what he had done.

'That was sweetly played, as ever,' said the queen, as my brother laid down his lyre. 'Come here, Ibrim.'

He rose and crossed the deck, unerringly,

to the source of her voice, kneeling down and bowing his face to the deck. She reached to one side. 'A token of our pleasure,' she said. And put the faience cat into his outstretched hands.

I felt the hairs rise on my head. I felt my father beside me stiffen like a scorpion, back arched. I saw my brother return to his hassock and cradle the cat tenderly in his lap, exploring its features with his delicate, musician's fingers: the paws, the haunches, the coiled tail, the pointed nose, the face. His fingers stopped at the unexpected roughness of the mud-clogged eyes, and, with two twists of the little finger, he pushed the two clay plugs inside, into the hollow body of the Nile-blue cat.

I leaped along that deck like a flying fish, snatched the figurine out of his hand and flung it over the side. As the Nile-blue cat sank beneath the bile-brown Nile, little black shapes wriggled away into the water, but only I saw them go.

There was a stunned silence. Ibrim felt about him, open-mouthed, appalled that someone had robbed him of his precious gift. Father slumped sideways against the cabin wall, as if asleep. I turned round to face the astonished gaze of the entire royal family.

'I'm sorry!' I gulped. 'I'm so sorry! But it was one of mine. I made it long ago. When I was an unbeliever in the one god! It was a likeness of Bast, you see! It was an idol to the goddess Bast. Not just a cat. An idol – an insult to Aten. I couldn't watch my brother kiss a pagan idol!'

Ibrim looked up to me, with his blind eyes, uncomprehending. Ankhesenpa-aten scowled at me, narrowing her painted eyes. But Nefernefruaten-Nefertiti inclined her head graciously and asked my father if he would care for a drink of water. The pharaoh reached out a hand and creamed some melted wax from his wife's shoulder to smear on his forehead. The mosquitoes were starting to bite.

I think such fear had gone through my father that all his hatred melted in the heat of it. He had almost killed his own son. Almost but not quite. Like that scented wax trickling in soothing drops down the royal skin, the relief cooled Harkhuf's incandescent brain and left only a kind of emptiness – a vacuum.

On the way home, we did not talk of anything that had happened, and Ibrim never was given a proper explanation. But when we got to the house, I straightaway presented Father with the stela I had carved for him. I believe my fear of him had also melted in the heat of the day.

He held it between his two hands as though I had just introduced him to his grandchild for the first time. Here was his promise of immortality. He looked from the stela to me, from me to the stela. 'I do not deserve this,' he said, fingering the figures of the gods, the hieroglyphs that spelt out his name, and he wept with pleasure.

His humility did not last for long. Soon he was considering the practicalities. How could it be got to Abydos? Who would set it up for him when he was dead? Who could be trusted with such a beautiful, such an exquisite work of art? That is how he described my handiwork! I thought my heart would crack. Not so much with pride, for I no longer craved his praise, but with a kind of aching tenderness.

'I shall take it there for you, Father,' I said.

He stared at me. Unspoken in his face was the knowledge that I did not believe in his gods, that I had gone over to the king's religion, that I was an Aten man. He did not hate me for it. He just did not entirely know me any more. 'Do you promise?' he asked, like a child seeking reassurance.

'I swear it, Father,' I said. 'It will stand there for ever, and your soul will travel there and be met by Osiris, Father of the Dead. By Aten, I swear it.' As I said it, I wondered what Aten would think, who was even then prising his way into our house with his flail of sunlight and crook of evening sunbeams.

9

Everlasting Life

All that was a lifetime ago. Several lifetimes, in fact. Akhenaten, divine prophet of the one true god, is long since dead, and sleeps in the Red Country, along with his eldest daughter Meritaten, and Harkhuf his animal collector.

Even Nefernefruaten-Nefertiti is dead now – the lovely Nefertiti, sphinx-like in her sadness, too, for she had loved her husband with a passion.

The lovely Ankhesenpa-aten married her half-brother Tutankh-aten who, at seven, became pharaoh over all Egypt, and wearer of the cobra crown.

I did not marry, myself, and I am glad of that now. These are dangerous times, and I should not like to see children of mine playing among the ruins of el-Amarna.

Only in one respect is Pharaoh Tutankh-aten like his father. He, too, changed his given name. To Tutankhamun. No longer is Aten sole god over Egypt. Tutankhamun has re-established all the old gods, restored all the old festivals. Now, when people talk about Akhenaten, they sneer and spit and curse his memory. They *all* call him 'the Great Criminal, the destroyer of gods'. I hear his tomb is smashed and looted, though the priests of Aten may have carried his body away in time and hidden it. I pray they did.

Tutankhamun has moved his court back to Thebes, to live in the palace of his ancestors, and el-Amarna is looked on as nothing more than a quarry, a source of bricks for new palaces, new temples to the old gods.

Some of us stayed on here. El-Amarna was our home, after all. But the priests of Amun are out to remove all trace of the Great Criminal and his consort queen. His altars have been smashed, his likeness disfigured in all the wall paintings. They smash his name and the name of Nefertiti wherever they can find them. They think that if they can keep the names from being spoken, they can ensure that the king and the queen will have no afterlife.

What do I believe? Sometimes, I think it doesn't matter much what you believe, so long as you never start to doubt it. I am a craftsman. I believe in beauty, and I know beauty when I see it. It was in Akhenaten and his life. It was in his temples open to the sky and his palace with its rooms full of the laughter of the princesses. Above all, it was in Nefertiti (*A Beautiful Woman is Come*).

They are out there now, those devout vandals, smashing his name, smashing hers. May the vandals themselves be swallowed up by everlasting darkness, as the desert swallows up their graves.

I can hear them getting closer, working their way through the city. That's why I've locked the door. Until they break it down – if they still have the energy – I shall go on working here, locked in my workshop. I am making, by the light of an oil lamp, cartouche after cartouche of the royal names. And do you see this head, I've made? This is a likeness of Queen Nefertiti as it is burned into my memory. So beautiful. So superhuman in her beauty.

Perhaps, they will break in here and smash my work as they have smashed so many works of mine over yonder in the palace. But while I have breath in me and light to see by, I shall go on speaking the names – *their* names – in stone, so that they may have everlasting life. A man must do what he can. While a name is remembered in this world, the spirit lives on in the Land of the West.

Am I a fool? One day the world will be a thousand years older, two thousand, three! Who then will remember Akhenaten or the divine Nefertiti? One thing I do know for certain! No one will remember me, Tutmose the potter, or speak my name aloud three thousand years from now.

When the ruins of el-Amarna were excavated, a beautiful carved head of Queen Nefertiti, as well as several cartouches of the names Nefernefruaten-Nefertiti and Akhenaten were found in a locked workshop. They had escaped both theft and destruction by the troops of the Pharaoh Tutankhamun.

Glossary

Beetling   Overhanging.

Boon   A royal favour or blessing.

Cataract   A series of river rapids and small waterfalls.

Coracle   A small roundish boat made of waterproofed animal hides stretched over a wicker frame.

Country of the West   Spirit world of the dead.

Dais   A raised platform, usually at the end of a large room or hall.

Electrum   A natural metal alloy of gold and silver.

Faience   Greenish-blue glazed pottery.

Flail and crook   Implement for threshing wheat and shepherd's curved staff, used as symbols of kingly power in ancient Egypt.

Ibis   A wading bird.

Kohl   Cosmetic powder used to darken around eyes.

Lapis lazuli   Brilliant blue semi-precious stone, much prized for inlay in jewellery.

Land of the West The spirit world of the dead.

Palanquin A covered seat built between two parallel rods. Used for conveying an important person, it is carried upon the shoulders of four men.

Pigment A powder used to add colour to a liquid.

Scree Loosely-piled, weathered rock fragments.

Serval cat A slender bush cat that has an orange-brown coat with black spots, large ears, and long legs.

Skiff A small reed boat propelled by oars.

Sphinx A statue with the body of a lion and the head of a man.

Stela (plural: stelae) A rectangular stone slab with a rounded top; inscribed with title, name and epithet (descriptive word) of the dead person; set up as an aid to secure continuing life after death.

Ushabti Small wood or faience figures put in a tomb to perform any tasks the gods may require of a dead person in the afterlife.

Historical Note

Akhenaten's capital of el-Amarna was uncovered by archaeologists in the 19th century and today, Akhenaten and his beautiful wife, Queen Nefertiti, are among the most famous of all the rulers of ancient Egypt. However, for many hundreds of years, the city's ruins lay forgotten and the pharaoh was virtually unknown.

For many people, the fascination with Akhenaten's reign lies in his dramatic and controversial religious reforms. Religion and ritual held a central place in the lives of ancient Egyptians and they traditionally worshipped many gods and goddesses. They believed that there were gods and goddesses responsible for every part of life, and death. There were those who created the world, some who brought the flood every year and others who took care of people after they died. There were also minor, local gods who were responsible for particular towns and places.

Each of the gods and goddesses had sacred animals that were linked to them. The gods could be represented in human or animal form, or as animal-headed humans. The first and most powerful of the gods was Amun. Amun was usually represented as a man wearing a headdress of two tall ostrich plumes, as a ram, or as a man with a ram's head. Likewise, Thoth, the god of writing and knowledge, was linked with baboons and ibises, and Bastet, the protective goddess, was symbolized by a cat. Worshippers could honour a god by making temple offerings of bronze or faience figurines of an animal associated with the god, or they could offer the mummified remains of the animal. Mummification was a successful business for the temples, which kept large breeding pens for animals. When they reached a certain age the creatures were killed and mummified, and the mummies sold to pilgrims.

Akhenaten was raised in a traditional ancient Egyptian manner. He grew up in the capital Thebes (modern-day Luxor) and worshipped Amun and the established gods.

Akhenaten came to the throne around 1353 BC and was crowned Amenhotep IV, meaning 'Amun is content'.

Soon after becoming pharaoh, Akhenaten rejected his royal name and his loyalty to Amun. He renamed himself Akhenaten, in honour of the sun-god Aten. The new pharaoh turned away from the old priests and forms of worship and began the cult of Aten the sun disc. Akhenaten declared that Aten was the only god. He banned the worship of the old gods and closed down sacred temples.

Akhenaten decided that the worship of Aten required a new location, away from places where traditional gods had been worshipped. He chose a site in Middle Egypt, along the Nile. There he build a new capital city which he called Akhetaten, 'Horizon of the Aten', which today is known as el-Amarna. To the east of the city, the pharaoh started preparing tombs for the royal family. On the plain near the river, massive temples to Aten were constructed. Unlike traditional temples these were open to the sun.

There is much we still do not know about this remarkable period in Egyptian history, including Akhenaten's reasons for his religious reforms. However, it is clear that Akhenaten's ideas were not accepted by most Egyptians. This was partly due to the powerful influence of tradition, but also because people must have found it more difficult to relate to this impersonal abstract god than their traditional deities.

Akhenaten's reign lasted 17 years and when he died the throne passed to young Tutankhaten, 'the living image of Aten'. This 'boy-king' later changed his name to the one he is known by today, Tutankhamun, 'the living image of Amun'. As he was still only a child, regents ruled Egypt on his behalf and they encouraged him to abandon the sole worship of Aten. All across Egypt, temples to the traditional gods were restored. It was not long before the new pharaoh left the city of el-Amarna and returned to the old capital. His subjects shut up their houses and followed him.

Later pharaohs attempted to erase all memory of Akhenaten's unorthodox reign.

Throughout Egypt his image and name were removed from monuments, his temples were dismantled and the stone reused for new buildings. The names of Akhenaten and his immediate successors were left out of official king-lists. His city crumbled back into the desert, vanishing as quickly as it had risen.

Map of Ancient Egypt

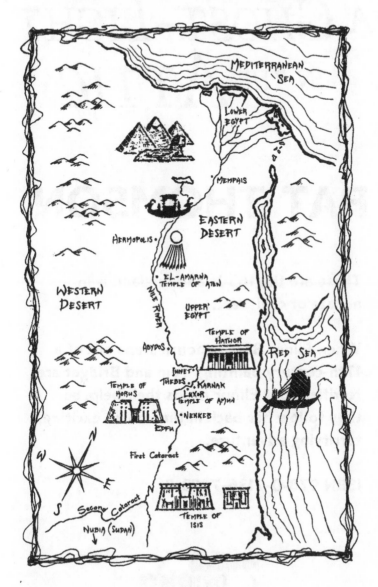

A GHOST-LIGHT IN THE ATTIC

PAT THOMSON

These are the 1650s and England is in
a state of civil war...

When Elinor Bassingbourn steps out of a
17th-century painting, Tom and Bridget are
terrified. But Elinor needs their help, so
they follow her back in time on an exciting,
terrifying adventure.

ISBN 978-0-7136-7453-8

ACROSS THE
ROMAN
WALL

THERESA BRESLIN

**The year is 397 and life in Roman
Britain is getting dangerous...**

**Marinetta is a Briton, Lucius is the nephew
of a Roman official. When they first meet
they hate each other. But when marauders
cross Hadrian's Wall they are forced to
work together.**

ISBN 978-0-7136-7456-9

A Candle in the Dark

ADÈLE GERAS

The year is 1938 and the world is poised on the brink of war...

Germany is a dangerous place for Jews. Clara and her little brother, Maxi, must leave behind everything they know and go to England to live with a family they have never met.

ISBN 978-0-7136-7454-5